OUR PLANET EARTH

Rain Forests

by Karen Latchana Kenney

BELLWETHER MEDIA • MINNEAPOLIS, MN

Blastoff! Readers are carefully developed by literacy experts to build reading stamina and move students toward fluency by combining standards-based content with developmentally appropriate text.

Level 1 provides the most support through repetition of high-frequency words, light text, predictable sentence patterns, and strong visual support.

Level 2 offers early readers a bit more challenge through varied sentences, increased text load, and text-supportive special features.

Level 3 advances early-fluent readers toward fluency through increased text load, less reliance on photos, advancing concepts, longer sentences, and more complex special features.

★ **Blastoff! Universe**

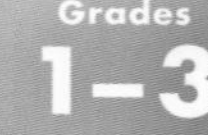

Reading Level

Grade K → Grades 1–3 → Grade 4

This edition first published in 2022 by Bellwether Media, Inc.

Library of Congress Cataloging-in-Publication Data

Names: Kenney, Karen Latchana, author.
Title: Rain forests / Karen Latchana Kenney.
Description: Minneapolis, MN : Bellwether Media, 2022. | Series: Blastoff! readers. Our planet Earth | Includes bibliographical references and index. | Audience: Ages 5-8 | Audience: Grades 2-3 |
Summary: "Simple text and full-color photography introduce beginning readers to rain forests. Developed by literacy experts for students in kindergarten through third grade"-- Provided by publisher.
Identifiers: LCCN 2021011413 (print) | LCCN 2021011414 (ebook) | ISBN 9781644875247 (library binding) | ISBN 9781648344923 (paperback) | ISBN 9781648344329 (ebook)
Subjects: LCSH: Rain forests--Juvenile literature.
Classification: LCC QH86 .K46 2022 (print) | LCC QH86 (ebook) | DDC 577.34--dc23
LC record available at https://lccn.loc.gov/2021011413
LC ebook record available at https://lccn.loc.gov/2021011414

Editor: Rebecca Sabelko Designer: Jeffrey Kollock

Printed in the United States of America, North Mankato, MN.

Table of Contents

What Are Rain Forests?

Rain forests are large forests filled with tall trees. They grow where rain falls often.

Almost every **continent** has rain forests. Many are **tropical**. Others are **temperate** and mostly located along coasts.

temperate rain forest

Rain forests receive the most rain of any **biome**! At least 60 inches (152 centimeters) fall each year!

Amazon Rain Forest

Famous For

- World's largest rain forest
- Home to 1 in 10 of the world's plant and animal species
- The Amazon River runs through the rain forest

Type

tropical

Rainfall

- Averages 120 inches (305 centimeters) per year

= Amazon Rain Forest

South America

Size

- 2,300,000 square miles (5,956,973 square kilometers)

Trees take in **carbon dioxide**. They also create clouds through **transpiration**. These actions keep Earth from getting too hot.

Rain forests have layers. At the very top, the **emergent** layer stretches upward.

The **canopy** is the roof of the rain forest. Huge trees block sunlight from shining into the layers below.

Smaller trees and shrubs grow in the **understory**. Vines climb up trunks and branches.

Hoh Rain Forest

Famous For

- World Heritage Site and Biosphere Reserve
- Located inside Olympic National Park

Type

temperate

Rainfall

- Averages 140 inches (356 centimeters) per year

Olympic National Park, Washington, United States

Size

- Olympic National Park: 1,442 square miles (3,735 square kilometers)

Few plants grow on the dark rain forest floor. Dead plants **decay** quickly. They provide food for animals and other plants.

Plants and Animals

tapir

About half of the world's animals and plants live in rain forests. In tropical rain forests, eagles fly between trees as they hunt sloths.

Tapirs grab leaves with their trunks. **Bromeliads** and orchids grow on trees.

In temperate rain forests, spruce and fir trees tower. Elk **herds** feed on **lichens** and ferns.

Salamanders and slugs crawl through dead trees and moss. Owls swoop down to catch flying squirrels.

People and Rain Forests

People all over the world benefit from rain forests.

Some medicines are made from rain forest plants. Foods like nuts, coffee beans, and bananas grow there. Some people groups live in rain forests, too.

Bena, a village of the Ngada people in Indonesia

Large areas of rain forest are being destroyed. People cut down trees to create farms and sell wood. This harms many animals.

Fewer trees are left to clean the air. The damage to rain forests worsens **climate change**.

How People Affect Rain Forests

- Cutting down trees for farming and wood harms animals

- Destroying rain forests worsens climate change

Keeping rain forests healthy can keep our planet clean. Important medicines will not run out. Plants and animals will stay safe.

Everyone can help by teaching others about rain forests. They are important to the planet!

Glossary

biome—a large area with certain plants, animals, and weather

bromeliads—tropical plants with short stems and stiff, spiny leaves

canopy—the rain forest layer located beneath the emergent layer; the canopy receives a lot of sunlight and rain.

carbon dioxide—a gas released into the air that is connected to climate change

climate change—a human-caused change in Earth's weather due to warming temperatures

continent—one of the seven main land areas on Earth

decay—to break down through natural processes

emergent—related to the top layer of a rain forest

herds—groups of elk that live and travel together

lichens—plantlike living things that grow on rocks and trees

temperate—related to a mild climate that does not have extreme heat or cold

transpiration—the process of plants releasing gas and water vapor into the air

tropical—related to places that are hot and humid year-round

understory—a layer of plants beneath the canopy of a rain forest